Andi's
Circle C Christmas

Circle C Beginnings Series

Circle C Beginnings

Andi's Circle C Christmas

Susan K. Marlow
Illustrated by Leslie Gammelgaard

Kregel
Publications

Andi's Circle C Christmas
©2011 by Susan K. Marlow

Illustrations ©2011 by Leslie Gammelgaard

Published by Kregel Publications, a division of Kregel, Inc.,
P.O. Box 2607, Grand Rapids, MI 49501.

ISBN 978-0-8254-4187-5

Printed in the United States of America
11 12 13 14 15 / 5 4 3 2 1

Contents

New Words

carpetbag an old-fashioned suitcase; a travel bag made out of carpet

company a guest in someone's home

fort an army base where soldiers live and work

hankie a square piece of cloth used for wiping the eyes or nose; a handkerchief

harness the straps and other gear that hold a horse to the buggy

hitch to connect a horse to a buggy so the horse can pull it

knit to use yarn to make things like a sweater or a scarf

rose water perfume that smells like roses

San Francisco a big city in California near the Pacific Ocean

spoil to let a child have his or her own way

Chapter 1

A Fly on a Leash

"Hold still, Andi," Riley said. "Hold really, really still."

Andi sat frozen. She stopped writing. She tried to stop breathing.

But that was hard to do.

"Do you see a rat?" she whispered.

A shiver went down her neck. Riley had seen a rat before. Right up here in the hayloft of the big barn.

Rats are disgusting, Andi thought.

"Shhh!" Riley said.

Then *thump!* Riley's hand came down on Andi's back.

"Gotcha!" he yelled.

Andi twisted around to see what her friend had.

Riley held up a fly.

"It's for your lizard," he said. "Pickles is probably tired of eating spiders."

"Are you going to hold it until we go inside?" Andi asked. "You can't write a Christmas list. Not with a fly in your hand."

"I know," Riley said. "Give me a piece of your hair."

Andi wrinkled her eyebrows. What was Riley up to now?

Most of the time, Andi liked Riley's ideas. But he had never asked her for a piece of hair before.

"What for?" she asked slowly.

"Never mind what for," Riley said. "Just give me one."

Andi didn't want to do what Riley told her. When Mother brushed Andi's hair, she sometimes yanked too hard by accident. That hurt. Andi sure didn't want to pull out any hair on purpose.

Not even one *teensy* piece of hair.

"Hurry up," Riley said. "I have to help Cook get supper. He'll skin me alive if I'm late."

Riley was right about that.

The ranch cook acted grumpy whenever Riley showed up late to help. Or forgot to do his chores. Or made a mess in the cookhouse.

"Oh, all right," Andi said at last.

She found a long hair that had come loose from her braids. Then she squeezed her eyes shut and yanked. "Ouch!"

Riley laughed. "Such a fuss over a tiny piece of hair. Now hold the fly and I'll tie it up."

Andi made a face and took the fly.

Riley worked fast. Soon the fly was tied to one end of Andi's hair.

Just like a dog on a leash.

Andi's eyes got big. She had never seen a fly on a leash before. It was buzzing around in circles, trying to get away.

But it could not get away. Andi's hair was stronger than the fly.

"Hold out your finger," Riley said. "I'll tie up the fly. Then you won't lose it."

Quick as a wink, he tied the hair around Andi's finger.

"When you feed Pickles, just break off the hair," Riley said. "Then toss the fly in."

"I bet nobody in my whole family has seen a fly tied up before," Andi said. "Where did you get this idea?"

Riley reached for his Christmas list. He picked up a pencil.

"One of the soldiers at the fort showed me," he said. "When I lived there before Mama got sick. Before I had to come here and live with Uncle Sid."

Riley began writing on his paper.

Andi didn't know what to say. Riley had been on the ranch a long time. Would his mother *ever* get well?

What if Mother got sick? Andi thought. *What if I had to go to the city and live with Aunt Rebecca?*

Andi shivered at that scary idea. She remembered seeing her aunt one time. It was right after Father died.

One time was enough.

Aunt Rebecca was old and grumpy. Andi did not want to live with her.

Not ever.

"That army fort is in San Francisco, right?" Andi asked.

Riley nodded.

"That's a long way away," Andi said. Then she gave Riley a big smile.

"But maybe you could visit your mother for Christmas. You could ride the train there. You can tell your mother about Cook. And how you do tricks on Midnight. And how we lasso the dogs."

Andi stopped talking. Riley was giving her an extra-big smile right back.

Like he knew something she didn't know.

"Uncle Sid is taking me to the fort for Christmas," Riley said. "He told me this morning."

"Hooray for your Uncle Sid!" Andi shouted.

Then Andi stopped shouting. She stopped smiling. Her happy thoughts about Riley turned sad.

She didn't want Riley to leave the ranch.

Not ever.

"Will you come back?" she asked in a small voice.

Riley was eight years old. Sometimes he acted too big for his britches. But Andi liked to play with him.

Riley gave Andi a friendly shove. "You goose! It's just for a visit. I'll be back."

Andi fell backward into the sweet-smelling hay. Even in December, the hayloft smelled like summertime. On rainy days, it was Andi's favorite place to play.

"Then hooray, *hooray!*" she hollered.

Chapter 2

Christmas Lists

"Don't squish the fly!" Riley said. "Tying it up was a lot of work."

Andi peeked at her finger. "The fly's still here. It's crawling around on the hay."

Riley scooted closer to Andi.

"I don't have much time," he said. "I thought you wanted me to help you spell words on your Christmas list. Let me see it."

Andi handed her list to Riley.

"Last year I got a gold coin in my stocking," she said. "I never even spent it. On account of that gold piece is a special treasure."

She grinned. "But this year I learned to write. So I made a *real* list."

Riley laughed.

15

"What's so funny?" Andi asked, scowling. She peeked at her list. "Did I spell the words right?"

SLiNG SHOt
~~LASu~~ LASSo
BRuSh for TAFFY
~~NIFE~~ KNiFe
HARMoNiCA
the OuTLAW RANgeR

"Sure, Andi," Riley said. "The words are spelled right. But . . ."

He laughed again.

"But what?"

Riley shook his head. "Do you really think you'll get a *knife* for Christmas? Or a slingshot? Or a harmonica?"

Andi snatched the list out of Riley's hand. "I might."

Riley snatched it back.

"Or *The Outlaw Ranger* dime novel?" He

laughed harder. "You copied that off *my* list. You can't read it."

"But you can read it to me," Andi said.

"Why don't you write down *girl* things?" Riley asked. "Like a doll and buggy. Or a new dress."

Andi jumped up and stomped her foot. It wasn't a very good stomp. The hay was too soft.

"You sound just like Melinda!" she huffed. "Her Christmas list is full of girl things. Dancing slippers. Hair ribbons. A book called *Little Women*."

Andi wrinkled her nose. "I think those things sound about as much fun as . . . as *watching a tree grow!*"

That was something Andi's big brother Chad said a lot.

Just then Andi heard a loud *clang, clang*.

Riley stood up. He handed Andi her list. "That's Cook. I have to go."

Andi stuffed her Christmas list in her pocket. Then she followed Riley down the ladder and out of the barn.

It was a gray, wet day. Raindrops plopped in mud puddles all over the yard. Andi wanted to splash in those mud puddles.

But she didn't have time to splash. The fly was buzzing around in her hand.

Andi stepped up on the back porch and went inside. She shut the door. Then she opened her hand.

Bzzzz! The fly flew in circles at the end of the hair.

"What on earth is *that*?"

Andi spun around.

Her big sister, Melinda, was standing in the kitchen, giggling.

"It's a fly," Andi told her. "Tied to a piece of my hair. I'm going to feed it to Pickles."

Melinda stopped giggling. She made a face. "Disgusting."

That's what Melinda always said about Andi's bugs and pets.

Then Melinda leaned close to Andi's ear.

"I'm knitting Mother a scarf for Christmas," she whispered. "Do you want to knit something for Mother too? Just from you?"

Andi's heart thumped. A surprise for Mother!

"I can maybe knit a pot holder," she said. "But I'm not very good at knitting."

"I'll help you," Melinda said. "Come up to my room after supper."

Andi nodded. Then she headed for the kitchen stove.

A wooden box sat behind the big, black cook stove. Pickles lived in that box.

It was too cold in the wintertime for Pickles to live in Andi's room. But it was warm and cozy next to the stove.

Just right for a blue belly lizard.

Andi picked up her lizard's box. It had a screen lid, so Pickles could have lots of air and light.

"I brought you a fly," she said.

The fly was sitting on Andi's finger. It looked tired from buzzing around so much.

Carefully, Andi set the box down. She held the fly and broke off the hair, just like Riley told her. She threw the fly into the box.

Then she closed the lid as fast as she could.

But Andi was not fast enough. The fly zipped away.

Uh-oh!

Mother did not like flies in her kitchen.

"Come on, Pickles," Andi said. "Let's get out of here."

Andi picked up her lizard. She put him in the bib pocket of her overalls. Pickles liked to sit in Andi's pocket and peek out. He was a well-behaved lizard.

Most of the time.

Andi hurried out of the kitchen.

Just then she heard a knock at the front door.

Andi stopped. Everybody on the ranch always went to the back door. Who would knock on the front door?

The knock came again, louder.

Andi skipped across the hallway and opened the door.

An old lady was standing on the porch. She held a large carpetbag in one hand. An umbrella hung over her other arm. Her wrinkly face was scowling.

Andi's stomach did a great big flip-flop. She didn't say anything. She just stared at the woman.

"Well, Andrea," a grumpy voice said, "aren't you going to invite your Aunt Rebecca inside?"

Chapter 3

Surprise!

Aunt Rebecca didn't wait for Andi to invite her in.

She stepped right into the house and shut the door. Her long, gray skirt swished against Andi.

Andi wrinkled her nose.

Aunt Rebecca smelled like a stuffy old room. A stuffy old room mixed with the strong smell of perfume.

Andi sneezed.

"Are you catching a cold, child?" Aunt Rebecca asked, frowning.

She dropped the carpetbag on the floor. Then she pulled out a handkerchief.

"Here's a hankie," she told Andi.

Andi did not take the hankie. She didn't answer Aunt Rebecca's question either. Her tongue was stuck.

And her eyes were glued on that fat carpetbag.

Oh, no! Andi thought. Her heart was thumping fast. *Is Auntie staying?*

Aunt Rebecca's foot started tapping the hallway floor.

"What is the matter?" she asked. "Cat got your tongue? Don't just stand there. Run along and tell your mother I'm—"

Just then Aunt Rebecca let out a loud screech.

"What . . . what . . . is that *thing*?" She pointed to Andi's pocket.

Andi looked down. Pickles was peeking over the edge of her pocket.

Uh-oh!

Quick as a wink, Andi pushed Pickles out of sight.

"Get rid of that animal this very instant," Aunt Rebecca said in a shaky voice.

Andi didn't move.

Aunt Rebecca kept talking. "After that I

want you to change out of those boy clothes and into a dress. You will not run around like a wild little boy. Not while I'm here."

Andi didn't say a word.

She wanted to. She wanted to say a *lot* of words. Like *Go home, Aunt Rebecca.* But the words would not come out.

That was a good thing. Those words were not polite.

Just then Mother came running. "What happened? Who screamed?"

Then she stopped and stared. "Rebecca!"

Aunt Rebecca made a *tsk, tsk* sound with her tongue.

"Elizabeth," she said, "when are you going to teach your little girl to be a *lady*?"

Mother didn't answer.

Instead, she smiled and said, "It's good to see you, Rebecca. But my goodness! What are you doing here? How long will you be staying?"

Andi thought those were really good questions. She stood next to Mother and held her hand.

Holding Mother's hand felt warm and safe. And she smelled good too. Like rose water.

Not like a stuffy old room.

"I am here to help you with the holidays," Aunt Rebecca said. "There is so much to do this time of year. Cooking, cleaning, baking. And helping with the girls."

Andi didn't like the sound of *that*.

Aunt Rebecca smoothed down her skirt.

"I rented a buggy and drove out here from the train station," she explained. "What a long, wet ride!"

Mother's eyebrows went up.

"Why didn't you tell us you were coming?" she asked. "One of the boys would have met you at the station."

Aunt Rebecca smiled. "I wanted to surprise you, my dear. And it looks like I did."

Then she scowled at Andi. "Why haven't you obeyed me yet, Andrea? I told you to get rid of that lizard and change your clothes."

Andi looked up at Mother.

"Don't look at her," Aunt Rebecca said. "I'm talking to you." She started tapping her foot again.

Mother gave Andi a tiny nod. She gently squeezed Andi's hand.

That meant, *Do what she says.*

"Yes, Auntie," Andi whispered. She felt a big lump in her throat.

Andi walked away, but she could still hear Aunt Rebecca. She was scolding Mother.

She scolded her about letting Andi keep a lizard.

She scolded her about Andi's overalls.

"The child has hay in her hair," Aunt Rebecca said. "And all over her clothes. The barn is no place for a little girl to play."

"She's been playing with her friend Riley," Mother explained. "There's no harm in that."

Aunt Rebecca snorted. "A fine thing, Elizabeth! Letting your little girl play with a *boy.* You must put a stop to that."

Andi covered her ears and ran. She didn't want to hear any more.

Aunt Rebecca was bossing Mother. A lot.

Pretty soon, Aunt Rebecca would be bossing Andi too.

Chapter 4

Supper Guest

The bossing started right away. It started at supper.

"Don't slouch, Andrea," Aunt Rebecca said. "Young ladies sit up straight and tall."

Andi sat up as straight and tall as she could. She felt stiff. As stiff as a fence post.

How can I eat sitting like this? she thought.

But Andi didn't ask that question out loud. It would not be polite. Children did not speak at the supper table.

Not when the grown-ups were talking.

For once, Andi was glad about that no-talking rule. She didn't want to talk at the table.

Not tonight.

Not with Aunt Rebecca sitting across from

her, watching everything with her sharp, black eyes.

Instead, Andi wanted to think. Thinking was easy to do with a no-talking rule.

Andi put a big chunk of roast beef in her mouth and started chewing. And thinking.

Aunt Rebecca is not the boss, she thought. *Why does Mother let her boss me?*

"Andrea!"

Aunt Rebecca's grumpy voice crashed into Andi's thoughts.

She swallowed her meat. "Yes, Auntie?"

"You are not eating like a lady," Aunt Rebecca scolded. "Ladies cut their food into small, dainty pieces. Like this."

Aunt Rebecca took a tiny bite of beef. It was about the size of a fly Pickles would eat.

Andi looked down at her own chunk of meat.

"It will take me hours and hours to cut it up that small," she said.

"Then you had best get started," Aunt Rebecca said.

Andi's stomach felt like a tight knot. She wasn't hungry anymore. She looked at Mother.

Mother shook her head. That meant, *Do as she asks.*

"Yes, Auntie," Andi said. She picked up her knife and fork.

A knife and fork were tricky to use. The fork always slipped. The knife always slid around.

Cutting her roast beef into tiny pieces was going to be impossible.

"Let me do it for you, honey," Andi's big brother Justin said. He smiled at her.

Andi smiled back. *Hooray for a big brother!* For sure Justin would rescue her from Auntie.

But Aunt Rebecca spoke up. "Don't spoil the child, Justin. How will she ever learn?"

Nobody said a word. Nobody talked back to Aunt Rebecca.

Not Justin. Not Mother. Not Melinda or Mitch.

Even bossy Chad was quiet.

Andi gulped. It looked like Aunt Rebecca could even boss grown-up brothers. And Mother.

She took a deep breath. "I can do it, Justin."

So Andi dug her fork into the meat. Then

she jabbed her knife into the big chunk and started sawing.

Andi's heart pounded. Angry shivers went up and down her arms. She would show Aunt Rebecca that she was not spoiled!

Back and forth Andi sawed.

Nobody paid any attention. Everybody was eating and talking. They were talking about cutting down a Christmas tree up in the mountains.

Andi did not even feel excited about that idea. She was too mad.

No fair! How come Aunt Rebecca can boss everybody?

Andi cut her meat faster and faster.

Just then Andi's fork slipped. Her knife slid out of her hand. It clattered across her plate.

Andi reached out fast to catch it.

But she missed and knocked over her milk instead.

Clunk! The glass fell on its side. Milk splashed out. It splashed all over Aunt Rebecca's plate.

Andi gasped.

Auntie yelped.

The plate was covered in a creamy, white lake. Tiny bits of food looked like little boats on the lake. Milk was dripping over the side.

It was a drippy mess.

Melinda's eyes opened wide. "Oh, my!" she whispered.

Mitch was coughing. It looked like something was stuck in his throat. But his eyes were twinkly. That meant he was laughing.

Andi wanted to laugh too.

Aunt Rebecca's face was bright red. She was fanning herself with a floppy napkin. She took deep breaths. She tried to talk.

But her words would not come out.

Then Andi looked at Mother.

Mother was not smiling. She did not tell Aunt Rebecca that a little spilled milk is nothing to fuss over. She didn't tell Andi there was no harm done.

"I'm sorry, Mother," Andi said in a small voice. "I didn't do it on purpose."

But Aunt Rebecca looks so funny!

She didn't say that part out loud.

Chapter 5

Who's the Boss?

Andi was glad when supper was finally over.

She helped carry her dishes to the kitchen. She peeked behind the stove at Pickles.

Then she ran upstairs as fast as she could.

Andi ducked into her sister's room. "Safe at last!"

Melinda took a key, put it in the keyhole, and locked the door.

"There," she said. "Now Mother can't walk in on our Christmas surprises."

Andi grinned. "And neither can Aunt Rebecca."

Melinda giggled.

Andi picked up her knitting needles and plopped down on the bed beside Melinda.

"These things are harder to use than a knife and fork," she said. "And they're slippery."

"If you go slow, you won't make mistakes," Melinda told her.

Then she showed Andi how to knit a pot holder.

Andi tried to knit slowly. She did not want to make mistakes. She wanted to do her best.

Only, it was no use.

Andi kept making mistakes. *Big* mistakes. Her fingers would not obey. She kept thinking about bossy Aunt Rebecca.

Finally, Andi dropped her knitting needles into the basket. *No more knitting tonight!*

"Melinda," she asked, "who's the boss of this house?"

"Mother is," Melinda said. "And sometimes Justin. And Chad bosses the ranch."

Andi nodded. "That's what I thought."

She let out a big breath. "So why does Mother let Aunt Rebecca boss me? She bosses Mother too. And Justin. Nobody talks back. Not even Chad."

Melinda put down the scarf she was knitting. She giggled.

"I don't know why Aunt Rebecca bosses Mother," Melinda said between giggles. "But I know why she bosses *you*."

Andi's eyebrows went up. "Tell me!"

"Aunt Rebecca wants to boss you into becoming a little lady."

"I don't need her to boss me," Andi said.

Melinda giggled louder. "Oh yes, you do.

You dumped milk all over Auntie's supper. And scared her half to death with Pickles. You wear overalls and climb trees. You're a *tomboy!*"

Andi crossed her arms and pouted. *Be quiet, giggle-box sister!*

"I guess Aunt Rebecca bosses everybody because she's our aunt," Melinda said. "And she's old. Old ladies tell everybody what to do."

"That's not fair!" Andi hollered.

"I know," Melinda said. She was not giggling now.

She kept talking. "I remember when Aunt Rebecca came for a visit a long time ago. She bossed everybody. Even Father."

Andi's eyes got big. "She bossed Father?"

This was bad news. If Aunt Rebecca could boss Father, then she could boss *everybody.*

"Aunt Rebecca was Father's older sister," Melinda said. "She thinks she knows the right way to do everything."

"*Mother* knows the right way to do everything," Andi said.

Melinda fell backward onto the bed. She let out a great big sigh and stared at the ceiling.

"You wait and see," she told Andi. "Mother will let Aunt Rebecca boss you. And me. And the boys. She's *company*. Nobody will talk back to her."

"*I* might," Andi huffed. "I might tell her she's not the boss of me. Or maybe I'll chase her with a spider."

Melinda sat up fast.

"Oh no, you won't, Andrea Rose Carter!" she said. "You won't *dare* talk back to Aunt Rebecca. Or do anything mean to her. Mother would be so ashamed."

Andi scrunched her face into a scowl. Her heart was thumping as fast as a galloping pony. Her eyes started to sting.

No crying!

Melinda put her arm around Andi.

"Listen, Andi," she said softly. "Christmas is Jesus' birthday. Remember?"

Andi sniffed. "I know that."

"Well," Melinda said, "you can't give Jesus a real present, like a pot holder."

Andi giggled. "'Course not."

"But you can give Him the present of trying to make Aunt Rebecca happy."

"How?" Andi asked. "She's always so grumpy."

"Don't fuss about wearing dresses," Melinda said. "Act like a little lady. Let Auntie boss you. Don't talk back. I think that would make her happy. And Mother too."

Melinda gave Andi a big smile. Like this was her best idea ever.

Andi slumped against her sister and stared at her lap. She didn't say a word.

"Well?" Melinda said. "Do you want to give Jesus that nice birthday present?"

Andi slid off the bed. She walked quietly to the door and unlocked it.

"I can try," she told Melinda. "But I think I would like to give Jesus a different present."

Then Andi opened the door and walked out.

Chapter 6

Mud and Coco

Andi opened her eyes. She peeked at the foot of her bed. Then she made a face.

That scratchy red dress is still here, she grouched to herself. *On my bed. Right where Auntie left it.*

A Christmas dress, Aunt Rebecca called it.

"I want you to keep this new dress clean," she told Andi the night before. "If that is even possible." Then Auntie had made a *tsk, tsk* sound with her tongue and left the room.

Andi did not want to get out of bed this morning. She had not wanted to get out of bed all week.

That's how long Aunt Rebecca had been visiting.

So far, it had been the longest week of Andi's life. She tried, but she could not do anything right. She could not make Aunt Rebecca happy.

Andi looked in the corner. Her overalls were jumbled up in a messy heap. She wanted to put them on and run outside to the barn. She wanted to hide in the hayloft.

Far away from Aunt Rebecca.

But she didn't do it.

Instead, Andi sat up and made another face at that scratchy red dress.

Then she sighed. She *wanted* to make her aunt happy. She wanted to please Mother. And she knew Jesus wanted that special present for His birthday.

Only, she needed help doing it.

Just then Andi got an idea. A *great* idea.

God is big, she thought. *He's bigger than Aunt Rebecca. He can help me do this.*

"Please help me give Jesus the birthday present of making Auntie happy," Andi prayed in a rush. She didn't even close her eyes. She was too busy looking at that dress.

Andi took a big breath and kept praying.

"Even if it means wearing a scratchy dress that I don't like one teensy bit."

Then she jumped out of bed and put on the dress—before she changed her mind.

When Andi sat down for breakfast, Aunt Rebecca said, "You look very nice, Andrea. But keep that dress clean today, do you hear?"

"Yes, Auntie," Andi said.

Then Aunt Rebecca frowned. "Why do you have a dirty rope hanging over the back of your chair?"

"It's my lasso," Andi explained. "Me and Riley are going to lasso the dogs. We're cowboys. Just like Chad and Mitch."

"Riley and *I*," Aunt Rebecca corrected. She shook her head. "No, Andrea. Lassoing dogs is not ladylike."

Andi felt her face get hot. But she did not talk back.

Instead, she remembered asking God to help her make Auntie happy. So she shut her lips tight and did not let any talking-back sneak out.

"It's not raining this morning," Aunt Rebecca said. "Would you like to show me your foal? Your mother told me she's very pretty."

Andi's eyes got big. She looked at Mother, who was smiling.

Hooray for Mother! Andi thought. Then she jumped up and hugged her.

"That's a jim-dandy idea, Mother," she said. "Your best idea ever!"

After breakfast Andi took Aunt Rebecca outside. She held her hand and skipped across the yard. Aunt Rebecca walked.

Andi talked about Taffy.

"She's the prettiest foal on the whole entire ranch," she said. "Wait till you see—"

Splash!

Andi skipped right through a puddle. Muddy water splattered her dress.

Mud splattered Aunt Rebecca's dress too.

Uh-oh!

"I'm sorry," Andi said. "I didn't see that puddle."

"Apparently not!" Aunt Rebecca looked down at her dress.

Then she shook her head. "Hurry and show me your horse," she grouched. "Then we must change out of these wet clothes."

Andi ran to the fence and whistled. Her whistle was not very good. Taffy didn't hear her.

"Taffy!" Andi hollered.

Taffy trotted up to the fence and whinnied. Andi's pony, Coco, trotted up to the fence too.

"My, my," Aunt Rebecca said. Her grouchy face turned smiley. "Your little horse is a beauty."

Andi beamed. Her heart felt full of love for her aunt. *Aunt Rebecca likes Taffy!*

"Taffy will be trained to pull a buggy, of course," Aunt Rebecca said.

Andi laughed. "Oh no, Auntie! I'm going to *ride* Taffy when she grows up."

Aunt Rebecca's eyes got squinty. She tapped her foot on the wet ground.

"Indeed you shall not," she said. "Young ladies do not ride horseback."

Andi's mouth fell open. Aunt Rebecca was wrong about that!

"Mother and Melinda ride horses," she tried to explain.

"Men and boys ride horses," Aunt Rebecca said. "A lady rides in a buggy."

Andi's heart pounded. She forgot her promise not to talk back. She forgot she was wearing a new dress.

"I can too ride!" Andi said. "I'll show you."

Before Aunt Rebecca could stop her, Andi crawled between the fence rails.

She ran to Coco and climbed up on his back. Then she gave him a little kick.

Coco started trotting.

"I can ride as good as any boy," Andi called. "No reins. No saddle. Watch me!"

Chapter 7

Riley

Andi trotted her pony along the fence. She trotted close to Aunt Rebecca.

"Look," Andi said. "I don't need a buggy. I can ride horseback just fine."

Aunt Rebecca jumped back.

"You're riding that muddy pony in your new dress," she said. "Get down right now! Do you hear me? Come out of there."

Uh-oh!

Andi made Coco stop. She slid off her pony and climbed over the fence. Then she jumped to the ground.

"I'm sorry, Auntie," she said. "I forgot about my dress."

Aunt Rebecca's face was red and scrunched

up. She was breathing hard. She shook her finger at Andi.

"For shame!" she scolded. "You're covered with horse hair and dirt. March back to the house and change your clothes."

Andi swallowed hard. Tears came into her eyes. She did not want to do what Aunt Rebecca said.

But she had to.

Just then Chad walked up. He was leading his horse and smiling.

"Good morning, Aunt Rebecca," he said in a cheery voice. "I need Andi to do something for me."

Chad did not wait for Aunt Rebecca to say yes or no.

He looked at Andi. "Run into the barn," he said. "See if any of the hens have hidden a nest in there."

Then he winked at Andi.

Andi zipped away from Aunt Rebecca as fast as a jackrabbit.

Hooray for a big brother!

No hen was sitting on a nest of eggs in the *wintertime!* But Auntie didn't know that.

Andi scrambled up the ladder into the hay-loft. This was one place Aunt Rebecca could not go. She was too old to climb a ladder.

Andi jumped in the hay with a happy sigh.

"Hey! What are you doing up here?"

Andi stopped jumping. Riley was sitting in a corner. His face was red. His eyes were red and puffy.

"What are *you* doing up here?" Andi asked. "Why are you crying?"

Riley rubbed his fists in his eyes. He sniffed.

"Did Cook skin you alive?" Andi asked.

When Cook was mad, he could really yell!

Riley shook his head. "Uncle Sid can't take me home to the fort, after all. And my pa is off fighting Indians. He can't come get me."

Riley shrugged. "So I won't get to see my mother for Christmas."

Not go home for Christmas? Poor Riley!

Andi sat down and patted his knee.

"Sorry, Riley," she said. "I'm sorry you can't go home. That's really sad. But you can have Christmas with us."

"Thanks," Riley said. But he still sounded sad.

"What are *you* doing up here?" he asked.

"Hiding from Aunt Rebecca."

Then Andi told Riley all about her grumpy aunt. And how she bossed everybody. And how Chad had rescued Andi from her.

Soon, Riley was wiping his eyes. He started to smile. Then he laughed.

"I wish I could have seen you trotting around in that new dress," he said, laughing hard. "And your aunt shaking her finger at you."

Andi laughed too. Riley always made her laugh.

In the middle of a chuckle, Riley stopped and pointed to a dusty corner.

"Hey, Andi," he said. "Look up there. Have you ever seen so many spiders in one place? I bet Pickles would love them."

Andi jumped up and ran to the corner. "Oh, my! Look at those things!"

Then she ran to the ladder. "Don't let them get away, Riley. I'll be right back."

Andi climbed down the ladder, raced out of the barn, and splashed through the mud puddles.

She ran into the house. Then she flew up the stairs to her room.

"Where is that jar?" she asked herself, panting.

Andi dropped to her hands and knees and peeked under her bed.

At last! She snatched the glass jar and shook it. Six or seven spiders bounced around in there.

She grinned. After today, Pickles would have plenty to eat for a long, long time.

Andi skipped down the stairs and headed for the back door.

"Andrea Rose!"

Aunt Rebecca's screechy voice stopped Andi in her tracks.

She spun around, holding the jar of spiders behind her. "Yes, Auntie?"

"Why haven't you changed your dress? It's . . ."

Aunt Rebecca stopped talking. She frowned. Her eyes got squinty. "What are you hiding behind your back?"

Andi's cheeks felt hot. Her heart thumped. She did not want to show Auntie the jar of spiders.

Aunt Rebecca might be afraid of spiders.

Andi backed up. One step . . . two steps.

Aunt Rebecca reached out and grabbed Andi's arm. "I asked you what you're hiding," she said in a growly voice.

Crash!

The jar slipped from Andi's hand and hit the floor. Glass went everywhere.

And so did the spiders.

Chapter 8

Buggy Ride

Aunt Rebecca saw the spiders and shrieked.

Andi shrieked louder. "My spiders! Pickles will starve!"

Melinda came running. "Get rid of those disgusting things!" she yelled.

Then Mother saw the mess. Her eyes opened wide. "What on *earth* happened?"

No one answered. Everybody was too busy shrieking.

Mother put one arm around Aunt Rebecca. She hugged Andi with her other arm.

"There's no harm in a few spiders," she said. Then she raised her voice. "And would everybody *please* stop hollering!"

Melinda stopped yelling.

Andi stopped shrieking.

Aunt Rebecca snorted. "Elizabeth, *when* are you going to teach your little girl to be a lady?"

Then she swished her skirt and hurried away.

Far away from the spiders.

Mother let out a long, tired sigh. She killed the spiders and swept up the mess. Then she told Andi to find another jar.

"There are more spiders in the barn," she said.

That made Andi feel a little better. She found a new jar and ran to the barn to catch spiders.

Before they all got away.

⤳ ⤝

Two days before Christmas, Melinda and Andi were baking cookies. All by themselves. It was quiet and cozy. And tasty.

Andi popped another warm cookie in her mouth.

Yummy!

But it didn't stay quiet for long.

Mother and Aunt Rebecca walked into the kitchen. Their arms were full of packages.

"Christmas surprises from town," Aunt Rebecca said, chuckling.

Melinda and Andi looked at each other in surprise. Grumpy Aunt Rebecca? Chuckling?

"I met a dear friend in town," Auntie said. "We planned a little tea party for this afternoon. A Christmas tea party."

Aunt Rebecca smiled at Andi.

Andi did not smile back. She did not know what to think about this chuckling, smiling aunt.

"She has a granddaughter just your age, Andrea," Aunt Rebecca said. "The four of us will have a lovely time. We can bring along some of the cookies you baked."

"Chad can hitch up the buggy," Mother said.

Andi didn't say anything. But she was thinking a lot. *Just Auntie and me? In the buggy? All the way to town?*

No, no, no!

She looked at Mother.

Mother smiled. That meant, *Yes, yes, yes.*

Later, Andi talked to Mother alone.

"I don't want to go," she said. "I try to make

59

Aunt Rebecca happy. But I can't do anything right. She doesn't like me."

Mother pulled Andi onto her lap. "Aunt Rebecca *loves* you, sweetheart. She's just not used to such a lively little girl. I want you to go with her."

Then Mother hugged Andi tight. "Can you do this for me?"

Andi did *not* want to do this for Mother. She wanted to make a fuss. She wanted to stay home.

But part of Andi's Christmas present to Jesus was pleasing Mother. She had told God that.

So Andi said yes.

She pulled on her scratchy red Christmas dress. Mother had washed it. And ironed it.

But it was still scratchy.

Andi put on her cape and a hat. Then she followed Aunt Rebecca out to the buggy.

The wind was blowing. Dark, wet clouds hung in the sky. The ground was muddy.

Pal looked cold and unhappy hitched up to the buggy.

But the horse did not look as cold and unhappy as Andi felt.

She shivered and watched Chad help Aunt Rebecca into the buggy.

"This is not a good day to be outside," Andi told Chad when he lifted her up on the buggy seat.

Chad just laughed. "Take care of Aunt Rebecca," he told her.

Then he waved good-bye.

Aunt Rebecca knew all about driving a horse and buggy.

Pal trotted through the puddles. He snorted and tossed his head. He didn't look unhappy now. He liked pulling the buggy.

It was a long way to town. Andi did not know what she was going to say to her aunt for all that time.

But Aunt Rebecca did all the talking.

She talked about her friend Mrs. Miller.

She talked about the Christmas tea party.

She talked about the cookies.

She talked about Mrs. Miller's grand-daughter, Emma.

Andi sat still and listened. Her eyes were getting sleepy.

"You know Emma, don't you?" Aunt Rebecca asked.

Andi opened her eyes. "I go to school with her," she said, yawning.

Then Auntie talked some more.

Andi stopped listening. Now she felt *really* sleepy. She was cold too. So she snuggled up close to Aunt Rebecca.

Aunt Rebecca smiled at Andi and kept talking.

Suddenly, the buggy gave a great big lurch.

Andi sat up fast. Her heart skipped. She grabbed Aunt Rebecca's arm.

"What's that?"

"Nothing," Aunt Rebecca said. "Buggies bounce around all the time. Probably just a hole in the road."

There was another big jerk . . . and a rattling sound. Then one corner of the buggy started to tip.

Andi yelped. She tried to hang on to the buggy seat, but it was too slippery. Over the side she went.

Splat! Andi landed in the mud. She wasn't hurt, and she was too surprised to cry.

Thud! Aunt Rebecca rolled out of the buggy and onto the road. She groaned.

A buggy wheel wobbled past, all by itself.

Then it tipped over and hit the ground with a loud *clunk*.

Chapter 9

Andi's Best Idea

Andi sat up and looked around.

Aunt Rebecca lay on the wet road. Her Sunday hat was hanging by a string. Her skirt was wet and muddy. So was her fur cape.

Very muddy.

Aunt Rebecca sat up. She held her head and moaned. When she saw Andi, she gasped.

"Oh, dear!" She took a shaky breath. "Are you . . . are you hurt, Andrea?"

Andi jumped up quick as a jack-in-the-box.

"Not a bit," she said. "I fell off Midnight once. That's Riley's horse. He's a lot higher up than this buggy."

She pointed to the buggy wheel. "The wheel came off. That was scary!"

"Indeed!" Aunt Rebecca said. "We must find the neighbors. They can help us put the wheel back on."

Neighbors?

Andi shook her head. "We don't have any neighbors."

"Don't be silly," Aunt Rebecca said. "Everybody has neighbors."

"Not us," Andi told her. "There's nobody out here."

Aunt Rebecca leaned against the crooked buggy. She took deep breaths. Then she looked up at the sky.

Andi looked up too.

The sky was gray, with big black clouds. A drop of water splashed Andi's face.

"It's going to rain," she said, rubbing the drop away. "I want to go home."

Aunt Rebecca sighed. "I know, dear."

But she didn't say anything else.

The wind made Andi shiver. Her clothes felt wet and cold. She waited for her aunt to tell her what to do.

For once, Andi wanted to be bossed.

But Aunt Rebecca didn't boss Andi. She

just kept looking around. And holding her head.

"Are you hurt?" Andi asked. Her stomach flip-flopped at that terrible thought!

"Just a little bump on the head," Aunt Rebecca told her.

Then she said, "We can stay here and wait for somebody to come by. Or we can start walking."

Andi's eyes got big at this news. "But, Auntie! We can't—"

"Don't talk back," Aunt Rebecca said.

Andi knew she shouldn't talk back. She had told God she would try to please her aunt. Besides, Auntie was a grown-up and knew best.

But maybe Aunt Rebecca's head was hurting too much to know best.

Andi's words rushed out before she could stop them.

"Nobody's going to come by," she said. "And it's too far to walk to town. It's too far to walk back to the ranch too. That would take a long, long time."

It would be dark before they got home. Andi didn't like the dark.

Not one teensy bit.

Aunt Rebecca's eyebrows went up. But she didn't scold Andi. Instead, she bit her lip.

"I forgot that we are not in the city," she said in a shaky voice. "There really is nothing out here, is there?"

"Just you and me and God," Andi said.

Just then Pal gave a little whinny.

Andi ran over to the horse and hugged him. "Pal's here too," she said.

That's when Andi got an idea. Her best idea ever!

"We can ride Pal home!" Andi shouted. "He's big and strong. And he's fast. He can take us home before it rains."

And before it gets dark, Andi thought to herself.

Aunt Rebecca's wrinkly face turned white, like she was afraid.

"No, indeed," she said. "A lady does not ride horseback. I would rather walk."

"But it's too far," Andi said. "You *have* to ride."

"I can't ride, and I'm too old to learn," Aunt Rebecca said.

Andi ran to her aunt and grabbed her hand. "You have to unhitch Pal. I'm too little to reach the harness. *Please*, Auntie."

"Yes," Aunt Rebecca said, "I can unhitch the horse. Then you can ride him home and bring back help."

Aunt Rebecca walked over to Pal. She unhooked the straps. They fell to the ground.

Soon, Pal was ready to ride.

"Come over here," Aunt Rebecca said. "I'll lift you up on the horse."

Andi took a deep breath. She was not going to do what her aunt told her. She was not going to leave Auntie all alone in the rain and mud. Especially if she was hurt.

And that was that.

Andi grabbed Pal's reins. She led the big horse next to the buggy.

"Climb up on the buggy," she told Aunt Rebecca. "It's a little wobbly, but you can do it. You can get on Pal. Then I'll get on. I know how to ride Pal. I can take us home."

"No, Andrea," Aunt Rebecca said. "You do as I tell you. I'll stay with the buggy. You ride for help."

Just then it started to rain. Cold, wet drops fell on Andi's head.

"It's raining!" she hollered. "Get on Pal! Hurry up, Aunt Rebecca! I want to go home."

Then Andi began to cry.

Chapter 10

Home for Christmas

Andi and Aunt Rebecca stood in the rain.

Andi could not stop crying. She did not want to be the boss.

But Aunt Rebecca was an old lady. She was wet and muddy. She was hurt.

Aunt Rebecca had to get up on Pal. She just had to!

"Please," Andi begged. "Get up on Pal."

"For goodness' sake, child. Stop crying," Aunt Rebecca grouched. "I'll get on the horse."

Aunt Rebecca pulled up her heavy skirt. She climbed on the crooked buggy. Then she slid onto Pal's wet, slippery back.

Aunt Rebecca shivered and looked down at Andi.

"You're very bossy for six years old," she said.

"I'm six-and-a-half," Andi said, holding up Pal's reins.

Aunt Rebecca took the reins. She looked ready to scold Andi for talking back.

But then her frown turned to a smile.

"Maybe you and I are more alike than you think, Andrea," she said. "You bossed me right up on this horse."

Andi rubbed away her tears. She giggled. That sounded funny . . . bossing Aunt Rebecca.

Andi climbed up on the buggy and onto Pal. She sat down in front of Aunt Rebecca.

"Reach around me and grab Pal's mane," Andi said. "I'll hold the reins."

Aunt Rebecca did what Andi told her.

Andi gave the horse a good, hard kick. "Let's go home, Pal."

Pal took off at a gallop.

Aunt Rebecca screamed. Her hat flew off. Her skirt flapped in the wind. She bounced and slid all over Pal.

But she did not fall off.

It was a cold, wet ride. Andi was glad when they finally galloped into the yard.

Chad and two cowboys were standing on the cookhouse porch, out of the rain.

"Chad!" Andi yelled. "The wheel came off the buggy. But I brought Aunt Rebecca home. She's hurt."

She yanked Pal to a stop right next to the cookhouse.

The horse stopped too fast.

Aunt Rebecca yelped and slid off Pal's back. Worse, she pulled Andi off with her.

Splash!

They landed in the middle of a big puddle.

Andi sat frozen. *Uh-oh!*

Aunt Rebecca was soaking wet. And muddy. And hurt.

And Chad and the men were laughing.

Auntie is going to scold me so much! Andi thought.

But Aunt Rebecca did not scold Andi. Instead, she started laughing too.

"You brought me home, Andrea," she said. "It was a wild ride, but you brought me home."

Then she kissed Andi's cheek. "Thank you."

Chad lifted Andi out of the puddle. "You're a mess," he said.

Then he grinned. "Good job."

One of the cowboys gave Aunt Rebecca a helping hand.

Andi hung onto Chad's neck and peeked back at Aunt Rebecca. She was walking slowly, like she hurt all over.

But at least Aunt Rebecca was not waiting in a broken buggy in the middle of a rainstorm.

She was home.

> <

On Christmas Eve, Andi held the angel tight in her hands. Up, up, up . . . Justin lifted her to the top of the tree.

"This is the best part of being the littlest," Andi said. "I get to put the angel on top."

"It's perfect," Melinda said when Andi set the angel in place.

As soon as Justin put her down, Andi stepped back to admire the Christmas tree.

Strings of popcorn wrapped around it. Paper cut-outs twirled. Tiny wrapped presents hid in the thick branches. Best of all, candy hung from ribbons all over the tree.

And the angel rested on top.

"I've never seen such a tree!" Riley told Andi.

He hung a star cookie from a branch. "I can't spend Christmas with my mother and father," he said. "But spending it with you and Uncle Sid is pretty nice."

He looked around. "Where *is* Uncle Sid?"

"He's gone to town for some last-minute gifts," Mother told Riley.

Andi pulled Riley down beside her. "Look." She pointed under the tree. "There are presents for you and me."

She whispered in Riley's ear, "I think one is a harmonica. It's just the right size."

"Andrea," Aunt Rebecca scolded from across the room. "No peeking under that tree." But her wrinkly face was smiling.

Just then there was a loud knock at the door.

"Anybody home?" Sid yelled. He walked right in.

"Look what I found at the train station," he said, smiling. "A special Christmas present for somebody."

Riley leaped up and ran across the room. "Mama!" He hugged her tight.

"Merry Christmas, Riley," his mother said softly. "I've missed you so much."

Andi's heart was doing happy thumps for Riley. She wanted to hug somebody too.

Right then Aunt Rebecca smiled at Andi. She held out her arms.

Andi dashed across the room and gave her aunt a great big hug.

"Merry Christmas, Auntie," she said. "I love you."

And happy birthday, Jesus!

A Peek into the Past

Boys and girls in 1874 loved Christmas just as much as children (and grown-ups) do today. Many families decorated their homes with evergreen branches, holly, and mistletoe. They used a lot of green and red colors for Christmas. Why? Green stood for the life they had in Jesus. Red stood for the blood Jesus shed on the cross.

Some families cut down Christmas trees to decorate. But they did not put electric lights on them. There was no electricity in 1874. Candles lit up the Christmas tree instead. But candles were dangerous, because they could catch the tree on fire.

Families made their own tree decorations. They strung popcorn and cranberries, cut out lacy paper snowflakes, and baked cookies. Candy, fruit, and nuts hung from every spare branch. Tiny wrapped gifts hid in the branches. Larger gifts were placed under the tree. A home-made angel usually sat at the very top of the tree.

Christmas centered around the Christ Child and children. Families sang Christmas carols to friends and neighbors. They went to church on Christmas Eve to remember Jesus' birth. Afterward, children hung their stockings for "Father Christmas" to fill.

On Christmas Day, families enjoyed sharing gifts and eating a big Christmas dinner . . . just like we do today.

Susan K. Marlow, like Andi, has an imagination that never stops! She enjoys teaching writing workshops, sharing what she's learned as a homeschooling mom, and relaxing on her 14-acre homestead in the great state of Washington.

Leslie Gammelgaard, blessed by the tall trees and flower gardens that surround her home in Washington state, finds inspiration for her artwork in the antics of her lively little granddaughter.

Grow Up with Andi!

Don't miss any of Andi's adventures in the Circle C Beginnings series

Andi's Pony Trouble
Andi's Indian Summer
Andi's Fair Surprise
Andi's Scary School Days
Andi's Lonely Little Foal
Andi's Circle C Christmas

And you can visit www.AndiandTaffy.com
for free coloring pages, learning activities,
puzzles you can do online, and more!